THE CLONE WARS™

FOLLOW THE FORCE

adapted by Rob Valois

Grosset & Dunlap
An Imprint of Penguin Group (USA) Inc.
LucasBooks

GROSSET & DUNLAP

Published by the Penguin Group

Penguin Group (USA) Inc., 375 Hudson Street, New York, New York 10014, USA

Penguin Group (Canada), 90 Eglinton Avenue East, Suite 700, Toronto, Ontario M4P 2Y3, Canada

(a division of Pearson Penguin Canada Inc.)

Penguin Books Ltd., 80 Strand, London WC2R 0RL, England

Penguin Group Ireland, 25 St. Stephen's Green, Dublin 2, Ireland

(a division of Penguin Books Ltd.)

Penguin Group (Australia), 250 Camberwell Road, Camberwell, Victoria 3124, Australia

(a division of Pearson Australia Group Pty. Ltd.)

Penguin Books India Pvt. Ltd., 11 Community Centre, Panchsheel Park, New Delhi—110 017, India

Penguin Group (NZ), 67 Apollo Drive, Rosedale, Auckland 0632, New Zealand

(a division of Pearson New Zealand Ltd.)

Penguin Books (South Africa) (Pty.) Ltd., 24 Sturdee Avenue,

Rosebank, Johannesburg 2196, South Africa

Penguin Books Ltd., Registered Offices:

80 Strand, London WC2R 0RL, England

This book is published in partnership with LucasBooks, a division of Lucasfilm Ltd.

ISBN 978-0-448-45614-0   10 9 8 7 6 5 4 3 2 1

The Jedi are the keepers of peace throughout the galaxy. It is their job to protect the citizens of the Galactic Republic against the threat of the evil Separatist Alliance.

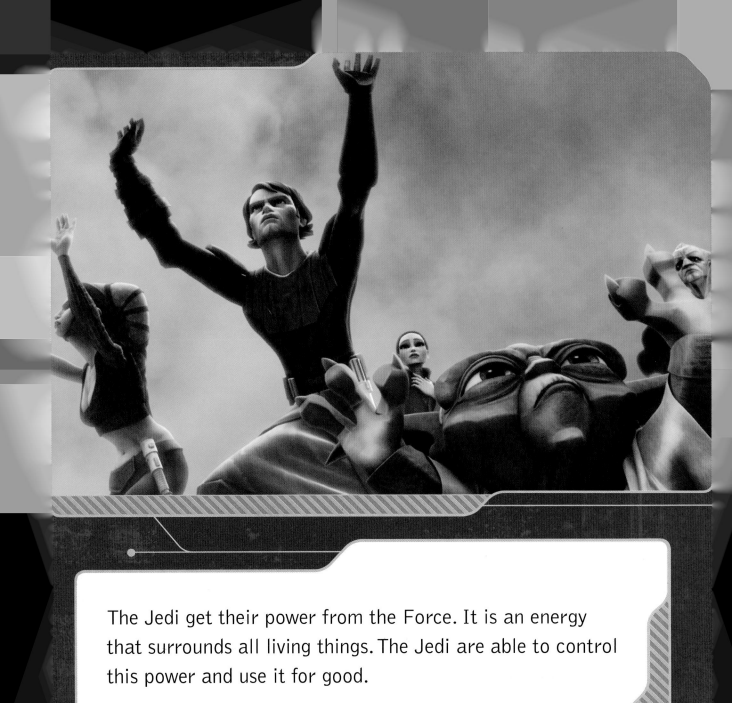

The Jedi get their power from the Force. It is an energy that surrounds all living things. The Jedi are able to control this power and use it for good.

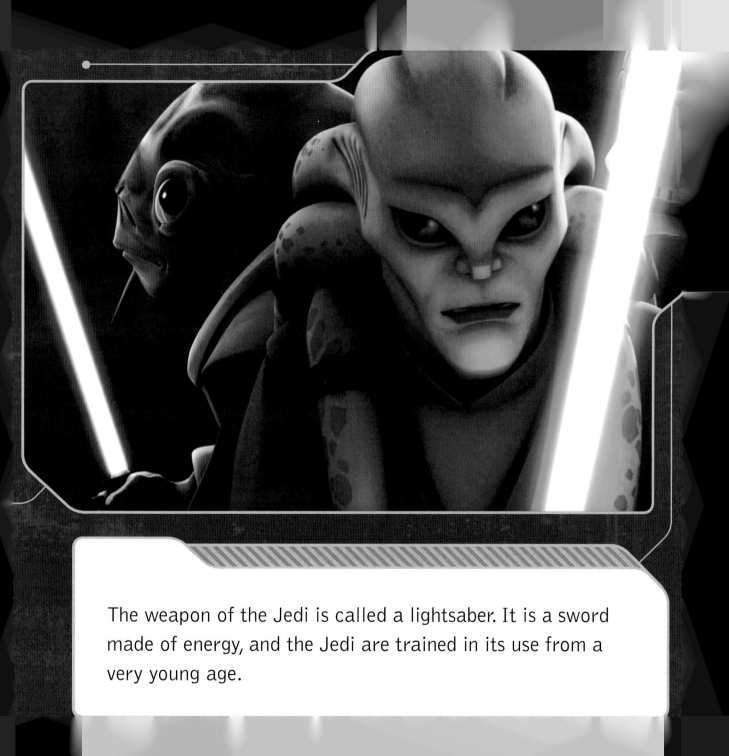

The weapon of the Jedi is called a lightsaber. It is a sword made of energy, and the Jedi are trained in its use from a very young age.

There are many Jedi spread out across the galaxy, defending it from evil—like Anakin Skywalker, a young, but powerful Jedi Knight . . .

And Obi-Wan Kenobi, who is a wise and experienced Jedi Master. Both he and Anakin are generals in the Grand Army of the Republic.

The Grand Army of the Republic is responsible for defending the galaxy from the Separatist Alliance's evil droid army.

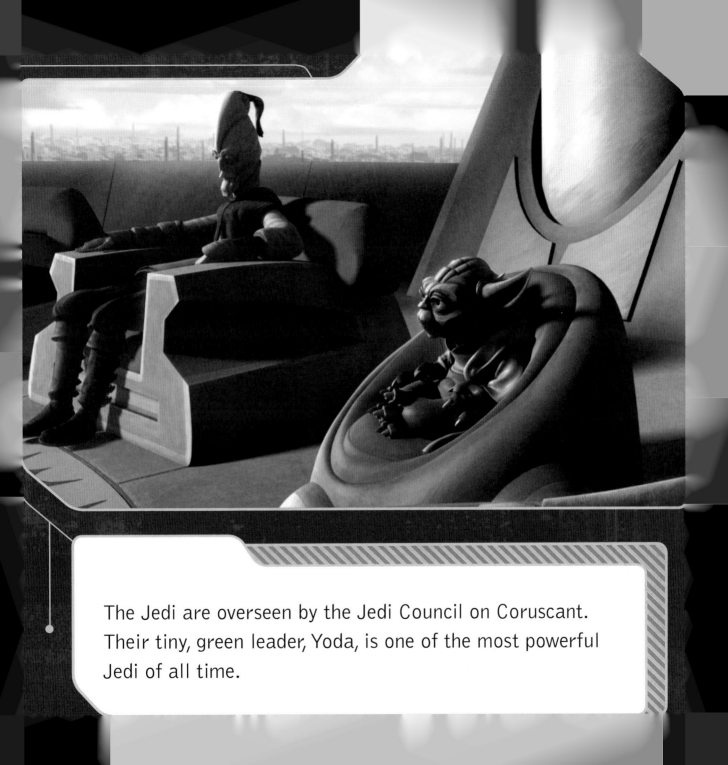

The Jedi are overseen by the Jedi Council on Coruscant. Their tiny, green leader, Yoda, is one of the most powerful Jedi of all time.

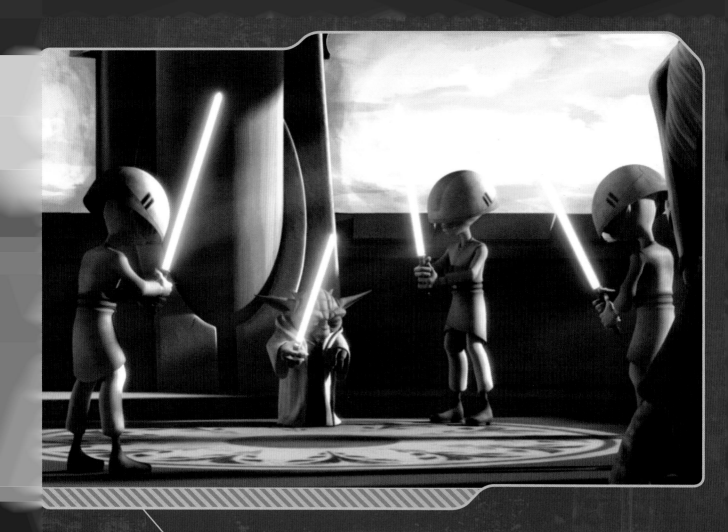

One of his main responsibilities is to oversee the training of the young Jedi in the ways of the Force. These younglings will one day become Jedi Knights.

Yoda is also the wisest of all the Jedi Masters. When the other Jedi have problems, they know that he is always there to help.

Ahsoka Tano is a Padawan. Padawans are Jedi learners who are trained by an older Jedi. Ahsoka's Master is Anakin.

Once Ahsoka was awakened from her sleep by a terrible dream. So she went to see Master Yoda to find out what the dream could mean.

Yoda was not surprised when she arrived. He was able to use the Force to sense her problem. "Troubled you are, Padawan?" he asked her.

"Yes, Master Yoda. I've been having dreams," she replied.
Ahsoka, like most Jedi, always felt better while talking
to Yoda.

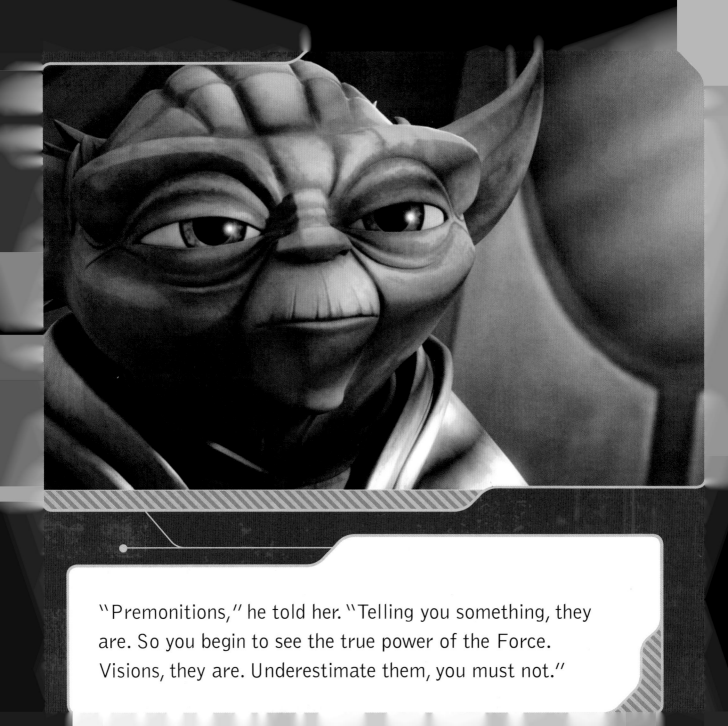

"Premonitions," he told her. "Telling you something, they are. So you begin to see the true power of the Force. Visions, they are. Underestimate them, you must not."

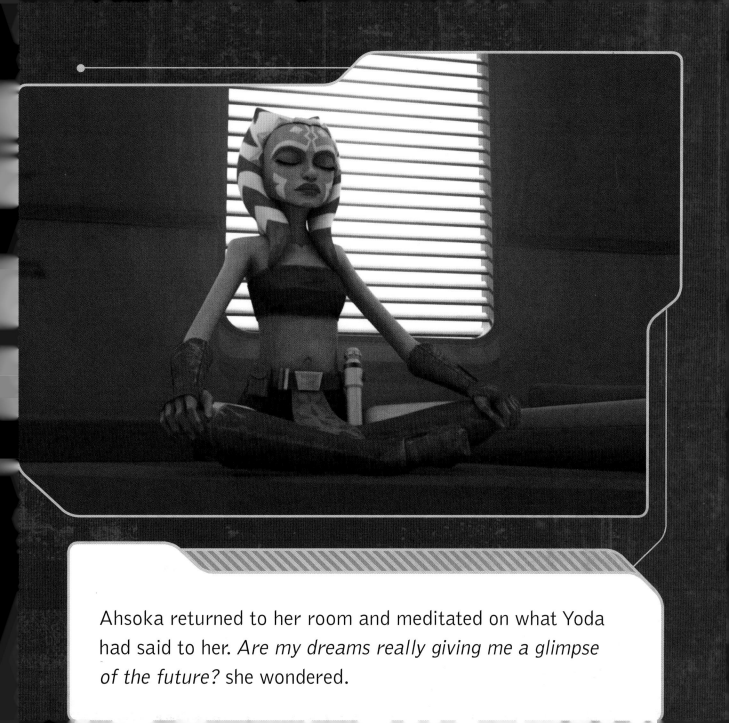

Ahsoka returned to her room and meditated on what Yoda had said to her. *Are my dreams really giving me a glimpse of the future?* she wondered.

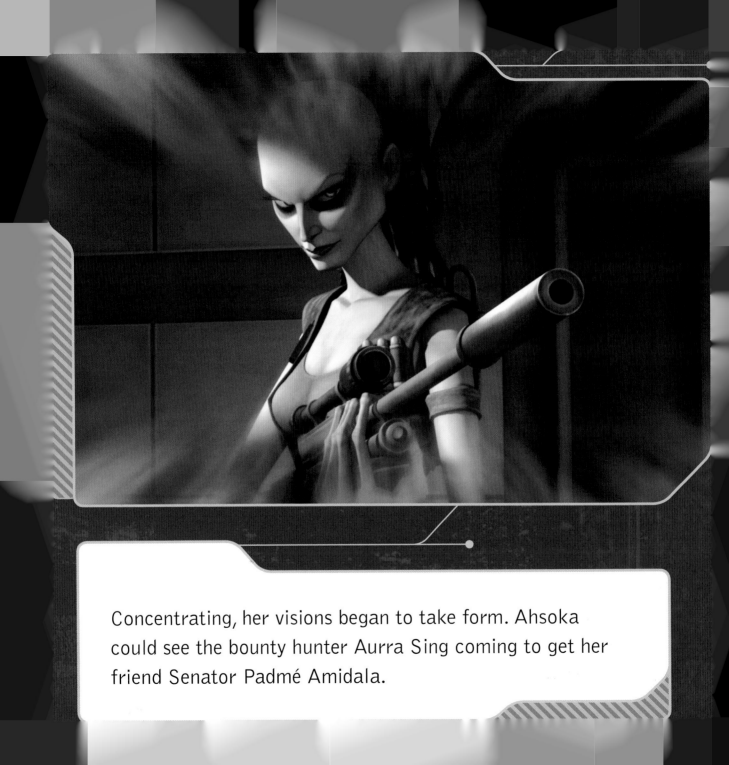

Concentrating, her visions began to take form. Ahsoka could see the bounty hunter Aurra Sing coming to get her friend Senator Padmé Amidala.

Ahsoka knew that her visions were warnings. Following the Force, Ahsoka rushed to her friend's aid. As always, Yoda was right.

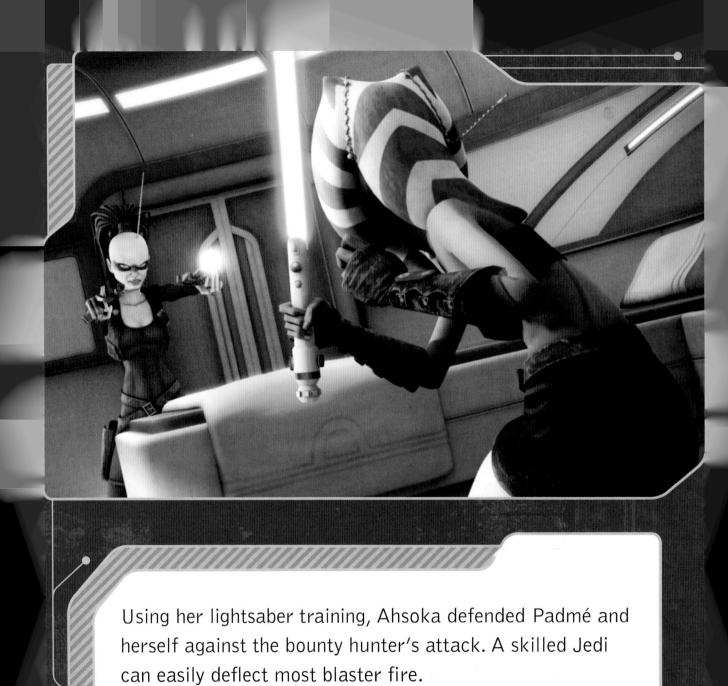

Using her lightsaber training, Ahsoka defended Padmé and herself against the bounty hunter's attack. A skilled Jedi can easily deflect most blaster fire.

Because of Yoda's guidance and her Jedi training, Ahsoka was able to harness the power of the Force and stop the bounty hunter before she could hurt her friend.

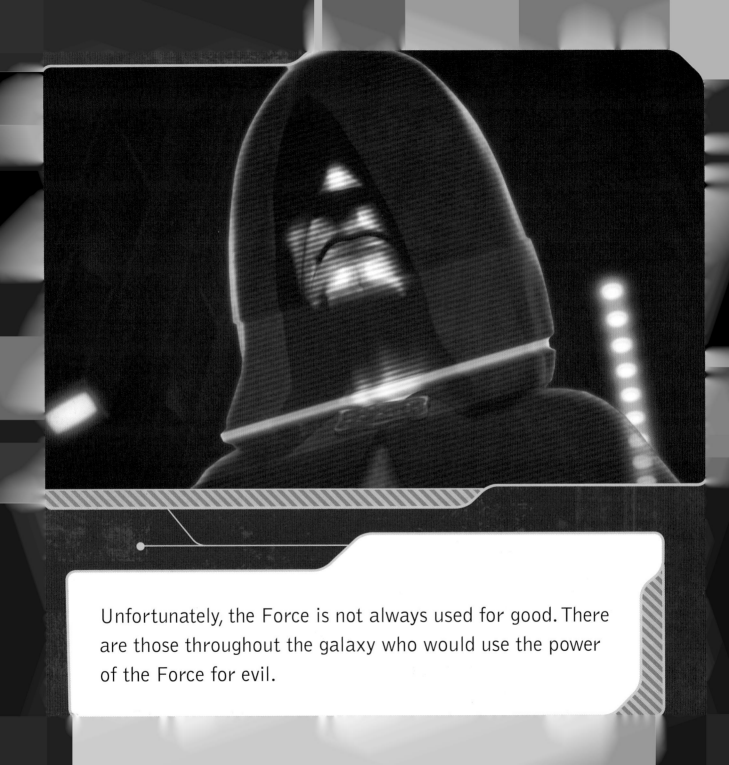

Unfortunately, the Force is not always used for good. There are those throughout the galaxy who would use the power of the Force for evil.

The villainous Count Dooku and his Master, Darth Sidious, are Sith Lords. Trained in the dark side of the Force, they will stop at nothing to defeat the Jedi.

The power of the dark side is based on pain and hatred. The Jedi are the only ones preventing the Sith from taking over the galaxy.

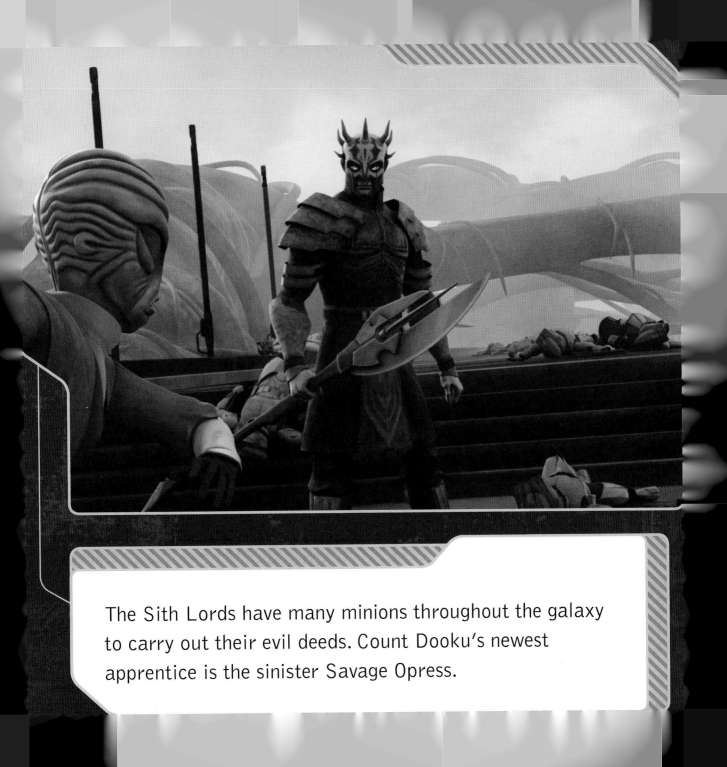

The Sith Lords have many minions throughout the galaxy to carry out their evil deeds. Count Dooku's newest apprentice is the sinister Savage Opress.

Savage was trained by the Sith to embrace the dark side. This powerful warrior has quickly become one of the most dangerous beings in the galaxy.

He replaced Dooku's previous apprentice, the assassin Asajj Ventress. Ventress is also highly skilled in the dark side.

She wasn't always a villain. Long before she embraced the dark side, Ventress was trained by a Jedi Master in the ways of the Force.

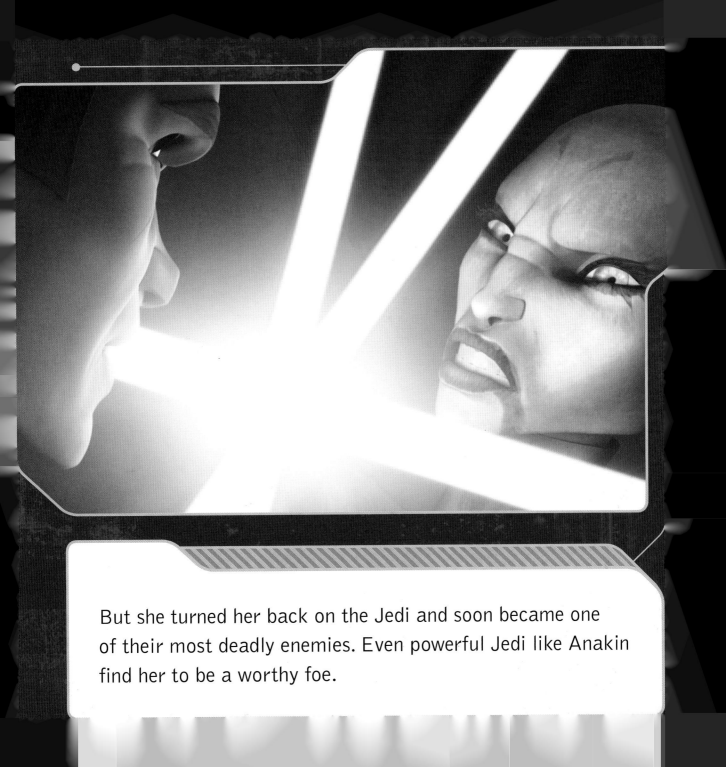

But she turned her back on the Jedi and soon became one of their most deadly enemies. Even powerful Jedi like Anakin find her to be a worthy foe.

But despite the threat of the dark side and their evil armies advancing throughout the galaxy, the Jedi will always stand strong on the side of good.

From one generation to the next, the ways of the Force and the teachings of the Jedi Order are passed from Master to student.

And despite all the danger and threats, one thing is certain: The Jedi are and will remain the protectors of the galaxy.